the Swan princess ™

Adapted by M.J. Carr
Based on a screenplay by Brian Nissen
From a story by
Richard Rich and Brian Nissen

SCHOLASTIC INC.
New York Toronto London Auckland Sydney

ISBN 0-590-22207-4
Copyright © 1994 by Nest Productions, Inc.
All rights reserved. Published by Scholastic Inc., 555 Broadway, New York, NY 10012,
by arrangement with Nest Productions, Inc.

Book designed by Dawn Antoniello

12 11 10 9 8 7 6 5 4 3 2 1   4 5 6 7 8 9/9

Printed in U.S.A.
First Scholastic printing, November 1994

Once upon a time, long years ago, there was a vast kingdom that had been smiled upon by fortune. The kingdom was ruled by a good king named William. It was blessed with peace and great prosperity.

When King William was quite old, he had an infant daughter named Odette. Because he had no other children, the little princess was the only heir to the King's throne.

As news of her birth spread, people came from miles around to present Odette with gifts. Queen Uberta, who ruled the neighboring kingdom, came with her young son, Derek. Derek laid a golden locket in the infant's cradle. As he did, King William caught Queen Uberta's eye. They had an idea. Perhaps, someday, Derek and Odette would fall in love. Perhaps, someday, the two kingdoms would be one.

In a far corner of the kingdom, deep in a dark lair, an evil sorcerer was brewing up another plan. His name was Rothbart. He wanted William's kingdom for himself. Rothbart conjured up a terrible, fiery magic. Flames leaped. Rothbart laughed. "The kingdom will be mine!" he cried.

Before Rothbart could work his evil magic, King William's soldiers discovered his lair. The King banished the sorcerer from the kingdom.

Rothbart left, but he swore revenge. "Someday I'll get back my power," he threatened. "And when I do, everything you own — and everything you love — will be mine!"

Time passed. Prince Derek grew older, as did Princess Odette. Each summer, the King and Queen brought the two children together. But the children didn't get along as the King and Queen had hoped. Derek preferred to play with his friend Bromley. Odette ran after the two older boys as they slipped off to play without her.

"Wait for me!" she shouted.

Then, one summer, Odette turned sixteen. Suddenly, Derek was struck by her beauty. It was as if Odette had grown from a gawky, young duckling into a graceful, sleek swan.

"You've grown so beautiful!" Derek exclaimed.

Odette was flattered. "Thank you," she said. Still, she wondered if the prince really liked her. "What else do you like about me?" she asked him frankly.

8

Though Derek wished to marry her, he couldn't think of anything else to say. Odette didn't want to marry someone who didn't truly love her. She said good-bye to Derek and mounted her horse to return to her kingdom. She and her father ventured off into the forest that stretched, dark and dangerous, beyond.

The royal travelers didn't get far. On a misty road a shadowy figure stepped in front of the carriage and blocked its way. It was Rothbart.

"Who goes there?" called the King.

His only answer was a flash of fire. Before the King's eyes, the dark figure transformed into a great, winged beast.

One of the coachmen escaped and stumbled back to the castle. "We were attacked!" he raised the alarm. "By a Great Animal!"

"Odette!" gasped Derek. He ran out into the forest to look for her. There, he found King William. The King was badly wounded.

"It's not what it seems," the King murmured weakly. He seemed to be trying to tell Derek something. Something important.

Derek saw a bit of gold glinting on the forest floor. It was the locket he had given Odette years before!

"Where's Odette?" he cried.

"Odette is gone," whispered the King.

Derek looked beyond at the vast stretch of forest. He was convinced that Odette was still alive.

Through the forest, beyond the trees, Odette was indeed alive. Rothbart had put her under a spell. He had turned the Princess into a swan and now held her captive on Swan Lake.

"Each day, when the moon sets," he explained, "you'll turn into a swan. You'll become human again only at night, when the moon rises. It's silvery light must cross the lake and touch your wings."

Beside the lake stood Rothbart's dungeon. It was made of stone and surrounded by a moat. Alligators swam in the moat, snapping and snarling.

"Marry me," Rothbart proposed to Odette. "Together we can rule your father's kingdom."

Odette shook her head defiantly. She would never marry Rothbart.

At the castle, Derek dreamed of Odette. He vowed to slay the Great Animal that had killed her father. Each day, Derek practiced his archery and hunting skills. His friends dressed up as animals. They scurried about so Derek and Bromley could practice chasing after wild, running beasts. One friend played a lion, another, a bear.

"Look ferocious!" Derek coached them.

Derek grew in skill and courage. He looked out at the thick tangle of woods in which Odette had disappeared.

"Don't lose hope, Odette," he whispered. "I'm going to find you."

14

That night, at Swan Lake, a full moon cast its white light on the water. Odette slipped up behind her two little friends, Jean-Bob and Speed.

Jean-Bob was a frog, who thought he was a prince. He puckered his green, frog lips. "Kiss me!" he said. He hoped that Odette's kiss would transform him.

Odette laughed at her funny friend. "Oh, Jean-Bob," she said, "you know the spell. I can only kiss the one I love. And he must make a vow of love and prove it to the world."

Suddenly, a big bird swooped down upon them. His name was Puffin and he seemed to be injured. An arrow was lodged in his wing! "Poor fellow," said Odette. She pulled out the arrow and bandaged his wing. Puffin was grateful.

"Now I owe you, Princess," he said. "And I will stay here until my debt is paid."

"Oh, I don't think you can help me." Odette sighed. "He put me under a spell."

"Who did?" asked Puffin.

As if in answer, Rothbart appeared. He doffed his hat and bowed to Odette. "Marry me," he proposed again.

"I'll never give you my father's kingdom!" Odette exclaimed.

Beyond them, the moon began to sink behind the soft blue hills that bordered Swan Lake. Dawn was breaking. The last bit of moonlight danced toward Odette. As the pale light shimmered and shone, Odette turned, once again, into a swan.

Though Derek still believed that Odette was alive, the others at the castle had given up hope long ago. Queen Uberta urged Derek to choose another princess to be his bride. The Queen was planning a ball. She invited all the young princesses from across the land.

Still, Derek searched the royal library. He paged through book after book, hoping to find a clue about the Great Animal that had killed King William. *It's not what it seems*, the King had said.

"What did he mean by that?" Derek wondered. "Of course!" Suddenly, the answer came to Derek. He rushed out of the library and through the front hall of the castle.

"Where are you going?" his mother cried.

"To find the Great Animal!"

"Don't forget!" his mother called after him. "Tomorrow night is the ball! Make sure that you're back here on time!"

On Swan Lake, Odette preened her feathers and stretched her long neck.

"If you want to see Derek," asked Puffin, "why don't you fly to him?"

"Because," explained Odette, "I have to be back here when the first glimmer of moonlight hits the lake. So I can turn human again."

That gave Puffin an idea. "I've got it!" he said, laying out his plan. "You could fly to Derek and lead him back here just as night begins to fall. Then he would see you turn back into a princess. Then he would know you are under a spell."

Odette had nothing to lose. "Let's do it!" she agreed.

"How about a little kiss before you leave?" begged Jean-Bob.

Odette shook her head at her foolish friend. She and Puffin flew off on their mission.

As they did, Derek and Bromley were galloping toward the forest as well. Derek was determined to find the Great Animal.

"I figured it out," he explained to Bromley. "The Great Animal is enchanted and can change his shape. At first, he may appear as harmless as a small animal, like a mouse. But without warning, he turns into the Great Animal. And then it's too late!"

Derek poised his bow, ready for attack. "He's here in the forest somewhere. I can feel it."

Just then, overhead, Odette and Puffin skimmed the tops of the trees. Bromley shot an arrow. It streaked past Odette and Puffin. Odette knew that Derek must be in the forest. She swooped down through the trees to find him.

Derek didn't know that the swan was Odette. She looked strikingly beautiful. Derek feared she might be the Great Animal in disguise! He threaded an arrow into his bow.

Phsssssst! The arrow whizzed toward Odette. "Come on!" Puffin urged. The two flew toward the orange, setting sun. Derek shielded his eyes against the bright rays. He kept the two in his sights and took off after them, leaving Bromley alone in the dense forest. Odette and Puffin flew back toward Swan Lake.

By the time Odette reached the lake, the sun had set. The first beams of moonlight shimmered across the water. Odette landed on the lake. Derek ran out of the forest and saw the swan. He raised his bow and took aim. But before he could shoot, the moonlight reached Odette and worked its magic. Before Derek's eyes, Odette turned back into a princess.

"Odette!" Derek cried. He rushed to her. "You're alive! I knew it!"

Just then, another voice rang out over the lake. *"Odette!"* It was Rothbart.

"You must go," Odette urged Derek.

"Come with me," Derek pleaded.

"I can't," explained Odette. "When the moon sets and the sun returns, I'll turn back into a swan."

"There must be some way to break the spell," Derek said.

"There is," said Odette. "You must make a vow of everlasting love and prove it to the world."

"How?" asked Derek. He had an idea. "At the ball," he said. "Tomorrow night! Come to the castle. I'll choose you and make a vow of everlasting love. In front of everyone!"

Derek tossed the golden locket to Odette.

"Tomorrow night!" Odette agreed.

Derek's visit had not escaped the watchful eye of Rothbart. "Thought you could fool me, did you?" he shouted at the Princess. Rothbart had found Derek's bow. He waved it at Odette, and flung it into the lake. Then he snatched the locket from her grasp.

"You won't attend the ball tomorrow night!" he taunted. "Have you forgotten? Tomorrow night, there is no moon!"

Without a moon, Odette would not turn back into a princess! At the hour of the ball, she would still be a swan!

Rothbart stormed back into his crumbling castle. He grabbed up the Hag who attended him. With a wave of his hand he transformed the Hag from an ugly witch into a beautiful enchantress, who looked exactly like Odette! Rothbart spun the enchantress around. "When Derek makes a vow of everlasting love," he said, "it won't be to Odette. It will be to you! Odette will die and the kingdom will be mine for the taking!"

Back at the castle, Derek and his mother bus-
tled about, getting ready for the ball. The royal
orchestra rehearsed.

"Where's Bromley?" Derek asked. "He's got to
be here. He's my best man!"

"You're going to get married?" asked his mother. Derek was too excited to explain. He caught
up his mother and waltzed her happily around
the room.

But Odette was not preparing for the ball, as Derek had hoped. That day, when she'd changed into a swan, Rothbart had seized her up and locked her in the dungeon. He threw someone else into the dungeon, too.

"Poor fellow got lost in the woods," he said. It was Bromley! "And now," Rothbart continued, "I'm afraid I have to leave. After all, I don't want to miss the ball!" Rothbart laughed an evil laugh. He slammed the iron bars shut.

31

Outside the dungeon, Puffin, Jean-Bob, and Speed plotted to help. Puffin had a strategy. He took charge.

"We'll find a hole in the dungeon wall," he told his friends. "We'll work at it and make it bigger so Odette can escape."

"But what about the alligators?" asked Jean-Bob. His thin, gangly frog legs were quaking. "We'll have to swim through the moat."

"Speed, you be the scout and distract them!" Puffin commanded. "Jean-Bob, you be the swimmer!"

The animals scrambled to their posts. They knew they had to work fast.

At the castle, the princesses were arriving for the ball. Derek watched expectantly, waiting for his bride. All the guests had now come. Where was Odette?

Suddenly, a loud knock sounded at the door. In stepped a young woman who had not been invited. As she turned to face the room, the Queen gasped.

"It can't be!" she said. The young woman looked exactly like Odette, though of course she was not. She was the enchantress. Derek took the girl's hand. The orchestra began to play.

Derek pulled the enchantress close to him. He waltzed her across the floor.

"Something about you seems... I don't know... different," he said.

The enchantress smiled slyly. "It's been so long," she said. "Don't worry. After tonight, everything will be all right." She handed Derek the locket. It must be Odette!

"Of course," Derek agreed.

Back at the moat, Jean-Bob, Speed, and Puffin worked as a team to rescue Odette. Puffin distracted the alligators, while Jean-Bob and Speed swam through the moat. The two swimmers found a hole in the base of the wall. They clawed at it to make it bigger. Soon it was large enough for Odette to squeeze through.

"We did it!" cried Jean-Bob. "Let's go!"

Odette plunged through the hole of the dungeon wall, into the murky water of the moat. The hungry alligators snapped at her tail as she swam.

"Go, Odette! Go!" cried Puffin. Odette streaked to the surface. She shook the water from her feathers and flew off toward the castle and the ball. There was no time to lose.

At the ball, the orchestra finished its song. Derek bowed to the enchantress. He called the crowd to gather around. "I have an announcement to make," he said.

Just then, Odette reached the castle. She peered into a window and saw Derek. Another young woman was standing at his side. The woman looked exactly like Odette! Odette beat her wings against the pane of glass.

"Kings and Queens, ladies and gentlemen...."
Derek was already making his announcement.
"Today I have found my bride."

Odette beat her wings harder against the glass.
"No, Derek!" she shouted. "It's a trick!" She flew
frantically from one window to the next.

But Derek didn't hear Odette. He continued his announcement. "Before you, and before the whole world, I now make a vow...." He turned to face the enchantress. "Of everlasting love." Outside the windows of the castle, Odette let out a cry of pain.

Suddenly, a cold wind whistled through the room. The ballroom doors flew open. In walked Rothbart. He laughed an evil laugh.

"You made a vow, all right," he said. "A vow of everlasting death!"

Rothbart pointed to the enchantress. As he did, she collapsed in a heap, and changed, once again, into the Hag. She leered up at Derek and cackled.

"Now Odette will die!" cried Rothbart.

Derek looked out the windows of the ballroom. He saw a feeble swan flying weakly from the castle. Derek ran out into the chill, moonless night. He leaped on his horse to follow her.

Odette struggled back to Swan Lake. There, she collapsed on the cold stone terrace. As she did, light sparkled and swirled around her, changing her from a swan back into a princess. Just then, Derek reached the lake. He rushed to Odette and took her in his arms. "Forgive me," he begged her. "It's you I love. The vow I made was for *you!*"

"Ha!" Rothbart appeared at his side.

"Don't let her die," Derek pleaded.

Rothbart waved his hand. Fire sparked. Light flashed. In a blinding display of his magic and power, Rothbart transformed himself from a man into an enormous beast. The beast had leathery, webbed wings, like a bat. His eyes gleamed a sickly yellow. His sharp talons flashed.

"The Great Animal!" gasped Derek.

The beast screeched. He swooped at Derek and sunk his talons into the Prince's shoulder. He caught Derek up in the sharp crook of his beak and flung the poor Prince against the ground.

"The bow!" Puffin shouted. "Derek's bow! In the lake!"

Jean-Bob and Speed dove into the lake to get the bow. They pulled it from the mud, and tossed it up to Derek. Derek caught the bow and reached behind him for an arrow. He had no sheath! No arrows!

Just in time, Bromley scrambled out of the dungeon. He tossed Derek an arrow. Quick as light, Derek strung the arrow in his bow. He shot it at the beast. The arrow pierced the beast's dark, evil heart. With a furious cry, the beast fell into the lake and died.

Derek rushed to Odette. She lay on the terrace, as cold and still as the stone. Derek cradled her in his arms. "Odette," he cried. Just then, Odette began to stir. Color flushed her face. Her eyelids fluttered and opened.

"Derek," she murmured.

"Oh, yes, Odette! It's me!" cried Derek.

Odette was alive! The spell had been broken!

Puffin grinned. He winked at Speed and Jean-Bob. "Well," he said happily. "There you have it. I guess Derek finally proved his love!"

Soon after, in the ballroom of the royal castle, Derek and Odette were wed. People came from miles around to attend the celebration.

Odette leaned over and gave Jean-Bob the kiss he had been waiting for. Jean-Bob tossed his cape over his shoulder. He believed that he was now a prince, though, as anyone could see, he had remained a frog. Jean-Bob strode regally into the crowd. "I shall now return to my rightful throne," he proclaimed.

As the orchestra played, Derek took Odette in
his arms. He waltzed her out of the ballroom and
into the light, fragrant air outside. Many years had
passed since the Prince and Princess had first
met. Many things had happened.

"Will you love me, Derek, until the day I die?"
asked Odette.

A flock of swans flew overhead.

"Much longer than that Odette," Derek
answered. He and Odette were at last united.
"Much, much longer."